Emma grew up in Thurrock where she was always labelled as a bookworm and always had a book or two on the go. After graduating in law at the University of Surrey, and marrying her best friend, they moved to Great Totham, where they now live and are raising their daughter. She has always had a lifetime wish to publish her own book and now prides herself that she can read her own book to her children, in the way that she has always dreamed.

Po the Pussycat's Big Day Out!

Emma Fuat

AUSTIN MACAULEY PUBLISHERS™
LONDON • CAMBRIDGE • NEW YORK • SHARJAH

Copyright © Emma Fuat 2023

The right of **Emma Fuat** to be identified as author of this work has been asserted by the author in accordance with sections 77 and 78 of the Copyright, Designs and Patents Act 1988.

All rights reserved. No part of this publication may be reproduced, stored in a retrieval system, or transmitted in any form or by any means, electronic, mechanical, photocopying, recording, or otherwise, without the prior permission of the publishers.

Any person who commits any unauthorised act in relation to this publication may be liable to criminal prosecution and civil claims for damages.

A CIP catalogue record for this title is available from the British Library.

ISBN 9781035813957 (Paperback)
ISBN 9781035814381 (ePub e-book)

www.austinmacauley.com

First Published 2023
Austin Macauley Publishers Ltd®
1 Canada Square
Canary Wharf
London
E14 5AA

iv

For Ela.

May you always grow up with Po by your side.

Po is an indoor cat. Black and white in colour and soft to touch. She eats, sleeps, plays and sleeps some more.

On a bright autumn day, she notices the windows have been left open. With the smell of fresh cut grass and the sound of fallen rustling leaves outside, she climbs up onto the side and shimmies herself out the window and into the front drive.

Wandering out onto the pavement, she sees many, many cars zooming by. Red cars, blue cars, black cars, white cars and yellow cars.

And oh, what's this?

It's Mr Toad.

'Mr Toad, I'm going to explore. Why don't you come with me? Don't be a bore!'

So off they went—Po the Pussycat and Terry the Toad.

Further down the way, they pass by the children on their way to school. Girls in checked dresses and boys in navy shorts and mums and dads in suits and uniform, ready to go to work.

And oh, what's this?

It's Mrs Ladybird.

'Mrs Ladybird, we're going to explore. Why don't you come with us? Don't be a bore!'

So off they went—Po the Pussycat, Terry the Toad and Laura the Ladybird.

They continued further, up the steep winding path until they came across a playground at the bottom of the hill. The playground had red swings, a yellow roundabout, a silver slide and a giant black zip line.

And oh, what's this?

It's Mr Wiggly Worm.

'Mr Wiggly Worm, we're going to explore. Why don't you come with us? Don't be a bore!'

So off they went—Po the Pussycat, Terry the Toad, Laura the Ladybird and William the Wiggly Worm.

They leave the park and make their way, continuing up the steep, winding path.

'Oh, this hard work,' says Po the Pussycat as she looks back. Her new friends are still with her; Terry is hopping, Laura is flapping her wings and William is slithering.

They turn the corner and clap eyes on a magnificent church. It has big gold bells, five stained-glass windows, one ginormous door and is surrounded by beautiful flowers.

And oh, what's this?

A humungous black raincloud has suddenly appeared.

Drip!

Drip!

Drip!

All of a sudden, the rain is coming fast and won't stop.

'I'm cold and wet,' says Po the Pussycat. '
This is no longer fun.'

They turn and make their way back.

Back past the beautiful church with the golden bells, stained-glass windows and gigantic door.

Back past the park with the red swings, yellow roundabout, silver slide and black zip line. William the Wiggly Worm returns home to his shelter behind the rocks.

Back past the school children, and their parents are now using giant, multi-coloured umbrellas to keep them dry from the rain. Laura the Ladybird rests in the cherry tree, using the leaves to keep her warm.

Back past the road with the red, blue, black, white and yellow cars. Terry the Toad perches on the lily pad in the neighbour's garden.

Back up the front drive, through the window and into the warm, dry house.

And oh, what's this?

A blanket by the fire.

Sounds Purrrr-fect to me, thinks Po.

THE END